PRIMITIVE

PRIM
ITIVE

cecelia rose

For my mom,

whose words of wisdom

I repeat to myself.

Carol Tankersley

1954 – 2020

Author's Note

I wrote *Primitive* after my mother died. In the first months of grief, I found myself remembering her humor, her generosity, the shadows she cast on the wall that told a story. Small, haunting, ordinary moments began to shape themselves into something like language.

This book emerged as a collection of emotional vignettes: rituals of care and silence, ruptures in family or identity, landscapes that echo the body. I wanted to write something that felt honest to the recursive strangeness of loss – how it refracts and reminds, and never resolves.

Some of these pieces are rooted in memory; others are imagined. All of them, in some way, speak to becoming a woman shaped by – and eventually separated from – the one who first held her.

Thank you for reading.

— Cecelia

Contents

Part III: Refrain

Part I: Relic

yellow-breasted chat

It was strange to walk up three flights in this old white
wooden building, fluorescent lights flickering and sunlight
barely penetrating the windows, and hear against all odds
in this virginal fortress the bright sound of birds with their
high-pitched lyric and unrelenting squeaks and squawks.

I imagined an aviary beyond the door down the hall, full of
red and yellow and green birds fluttering against the walls
and filthy panes, stray light beams reflecting off their
glossy sheen, their wings rowing glowing particles of dust
into the dim, their exotic and elated cries ringing through
the vents.

The walnut floors were warped and they whined with
every footstep. Peeling paint exposed damp oak doors.
Narrow halls held thin windows through which you could
admire the persistence of iron gates.

Do you marvel at the building's life, how it is like an
organism unto itself, how it breathes and guides and

corners, envelopes and yearns, or do you run like a cat out of the rain?

The sound of canaries and wrens, or quetzals and kingfishers, was a paradise where mural mountains met the sea and doorknobs shone like golden eggs.

I turned away but pitied their restraints.

mother shadow

Shadow puppet bird: pointer and middle finger pressed together atop thumb, ring and pinky fingers folded in.

It bobs its head up and down for "yes" and tilts its gaze toward the ceiling inquisitively, as if it just heard the sound of another chickee bird nearby. It lowers its face in despair if it feels it isn't liked.

The chickee bird lives on red rose curtains chilled by the night breeze that I cannot see, but feel, like the shadow that I cannot touch, but love.

may day

Every May we drove to a village in northern Wisconsin,
passing a thousand shades of green where glaciers used to
be.

The county was known for timber and every few miles
logs were piled into a ziggurat, some with a Celtic blue dot
painted in their middle. Properties had Fraktur surnames
on their mailboxes or hex signs on their barns.

She commented on the abundance of trillium in the
woods, the delicate tri-petaled white flower multiplying
before us as we walked through the shade into a clearing.

We stood in a Victorian ruff of evergreens when she told
me she spent her younger Mays on a dock catching bluegill
in a bird cage.

In the same way you cannot move a hurt animal without
causing further harm, you cannot visit the ghost of your
mother.

A hurt animal mourns their mother who mourns their
mother who mourns their mother in May.

half-moon over alma

We made believe we lived in her dream home. We called the brown front door French doors and the windows bay windows, and we sat on the Persian rug in the center of the living room eating Golden Delicious mangoes from Manila.

Alma would cry rivers that flowed down the hall toward the patio to drain. The next day, birds would be singing and the house would seem brighter, lit by an internal sun that cast no shadows, glinting off the windchimes and silverware, all geraniums and happiness, having been filled with sorrow, unleashing all of it upon her environment, and being glad in the subsequent lightness of mind.

When the windows were open, the spider webs anchored in the ceilings floated softly in and out, like white lace curtains billowing in an ocean breeze, and she told me the best women have great luck with emptiness.

pry

The tile floor of the Wright home was scuffed by chairs that held a father, a mother, and their two children. The dinner table was amber shellacked pine and the walls were seafoam green with a die-cut border of cherries, pears, apples, and grapes.

There were rules for dinner-table decorum:

1. You must say grace.

   "Father, bless this food to the nourishment of our bodies and us to thy service, and keep us ever mindful of the needs of others. In Jesus' name, Amen."

2. You must finish all the food on your plate. Eating all your food is a sign of respect. Failing to eat all your food is a sign of disrespect.

3. You must share two good things and one bad thing that happened that day.

The disclosure was to occur in clockwise rotation beginning with the father, proceeding to the mother, then the son, then the daughter.

On the TV, MSNBC News reported that Princess Diana was seriously injured in a high-speed collision.

Grace concluded, the father told the table in chipper tones that he called his father who was doing well, had a successful meeting with a vendor, and hit traffic on the way to work.

Brian Williams read a bulletin from another news station that Princess Diana had died.

The mother's cheeks flushed as she told her family she had enjoyed the songs on the radio that day, finished a challenging aerobics class, and ate too much for lunch.

Buckingham Palace confirmed Princess Diana's death.

The son shared that he received a letter from his pen pal, got a job tutoring math, and would have less time to play video games.

The front end of the Mercedes Benz sedan was unrecognizable.

That afternoon, the daughter had been caught scantily clad in a changing room by a janitor who took a moment's liberty before getting back to work.

"I don't have anything to share today."

The father clenched his teeth.

"If you don't have two good things to share, which you should, you can finish dinner and leave. And if you can't be grateful," he gave her additional servings of fried chicken, mashed potatoes, and peas as he spoke, "I'll prise open your mouth and stroke your throat like we did on the farm."

Geese and ducks and suffragettes danced before her eyes, the force-fed of now and then.

She fixed her eyes on the wall behind her mother, where the cherries had started to peel.

"I made breakfast, finished a book, and forgot my lines in rehearsal."

"Good."

Colossians 3:20 – *Children, obey your parents in everything, for this pleases the Lord.*

maggie, martha

He offered her a pat of butter on the tip of his knife. She took it and slowly cracked it in half before scraping it on her toast. They sat in silence at the breakfast table until she commented on the variety of birds in the birches outside the window. He reached over to take her hand and say he was the happiest man on earth.

Martha once adored the hyperbole that had by now grown stale. His nickname for her was Maggie and she had begun to suspect an affair with a younger, brighter version of herself. Still, they sat and held hands over the table they built together, next to their Siamese cat Doc, in their Colonial Revival home in Bangor, Maine.

"Goodbye, love."

They held each other tight. Joe's hands were rough and calloused with long tapered fingers and strong wrists, forearms that could easily lift her and shoulders onto which wisps of greying brown hair fell. His days at the coast were growing longer as the shadows on the wall grew shorter, signaling spring.

Then a creak of hinges, a beam of sunlight, a car door slamming.

Martha traced a spalted maple ripple on the table and removed the china whose cobalt ridges cradled crumbs.

It was a pleasant morning and the sun cast a gleam on the countertops. A cool draft from the open window caressed the "dancing-lady" orchid on the sill. She tied a cotton bandana around her head with a neat knot at the top.

The porcelain was stacked with care and placed gently in the sink with dishes from the day before. She began to scrub.

Her hands were soapy and warm when she picked up a fistful of knives.

I am a woman in a house with a man.

Outside the window, the petals of purple bearded iris were weighed down by dew and brushed ambitious leaves beneath. Just the other day, it seemed, she was a girl walking beside her bloodhound Hyppa in the backyard. Her patio was encircled by ravaged gourds, and in a ring

around the ravaged gourds were the bodies of raccoons or
possums or squirrels her father had shot. The more the
gourds decomposed, the greater number of animals visited,
the greater number of bodies. When their own flesh
decomposed, she took the skulls and buried them
methodically across the property – under grapevines, along
the creek, on a strawberry-lined path. With her keen nose
and eager paws, Hyppa found every skull.

Martha dried her hands and inhaled the fragrant breeze
that swept across a bed of hyacinths.

Symphonies must be written in the kitchen, when you're doing dishes.

She stacked the saucers and put them away, recalling
indigo-stained hands from picking blackberries, when the
juice bled into the creases of her palms.

...

Her husband's effects were strewn throughout the house,
his gold-plated watch here and spare change there, a few
cough drops and a pen.

These are the things of a wonderful man.

While he was observing the behavior of tides and currents at Belfast Bay, she grabbed the handful of change and the rest of his things from the coffee table and put them in his nightstand, pausing to look at the framed photo of their first Christmas together. She wore the same burgundy sweater that morning that she had worn in the photo, and his eyes were the same shade blue as the cat's.

Spare drift cards were placed in his desk drawer atop current charts and she ran her hands along the black lines that so minutely travelled. Doc jumped on the desk to nuzzle her hand before galloping into the hallway and perching on the demilune beside a vase of heavy roses, carefully biting the leaves that tickled his nose. Above the blooms, a navy sign with white calligraphy read:

Get on, get honor, get honest.

"Whatcha thinking, Doc? Want a bath?" was met with a disapproving gaze.

Martha was on sabbatical and had begun to feel her body ache, particularly her rib cage, as if a corset was restricting her breath. She ran a salt bath and stripped off her clothes to the tune of *Liebestraum.*

Her red toenails floated in the cool water. As the melody of No. 3 swelled, she played along on the surface of the water, moving decisively from one key to the next. The drops left her fingers hesitantly as they met water once more, recycled to a new note. It was such work to absorb the silence in her home. And in an old home, silence moves in great waves.

O love, so long as you can!

She got out of the tub and pulled a large towel around herself.

"Get dressed, dry hair, feed Doc," she repeated to herself. Then it was, "clean bedding, clean towels, clean clothes," and "empty litter box, sweep, take out garbage," and "repot orchid, bring in firewood, call roofer," and "read news, make dinner, set table." The sun considered setting when she was done.

Grabbing clean sheets, she made the bed with each corner forcefully stretched and smoothed, tucking flannel wings securely under the mattress. Wrinkles were pulled taut before she fell asleep on her stomach, covered in a still-damp quilt.

Sleep came like the tide and, in it, her bones thickened. A low rumble sounded in deep-sea trenches and her body transformed into that of a blue whale. The weight of the water held her tight. Her heart beat loudly inside of her and its vibrations sprang out, meeting the trembling song of another. A wall of glass, impassable save for a small opening, appeared beside her, and she saw the hazy outline of a mammoth blue body approaching her own. They faced each other in the dim and contemplated the opening between them. It was, perhaps, too small to pass through.

…

The sound of spare change, a cough drop, and a pen dropped onto a table nudged her half awake. His body beside hers, then gone.

Daylight called her eyes to open like the cry of Doc might have. The bare expanse of wall before her was a prism of pale greys and pearl. This morning's radiance turned their typically austere home into a coastal cottage with artful shadows and golden specks of dust floating toward the fireplace. Her body was still heavy like the decorative steel anchor on the mantel. She looked for the purple bearded iris outside her window, now lying on the ground in a broken bouquet.

Doc jumped on the breakfast table and blue eyes under a brown mask met her own.

"Morning, Doc."

She tied a bandana around her hair. Joe's raincoat was hung in the closet and a small notebook, a drift bottle, and a novel were set on his desk. In that moment, she imagined him in the boat off the bay, setting pink drift cards delicately into the water as if they were petals and watching them float away with the current.

Her fingers traced the reflections of light around dirty glasses left by the sink. His reading glasses were returned to their case. Everything in its place.

Mist blanketed that afternoon and evening. As rain began to pelt the sides of the house and rattle the windows, the door opened and Joe walked in, shedding his wet jacket and bag in the foyer.

"Maggie! I'm home for the day," he said as he gave her a hug and picked her up in his arms. "Bad storm brewing off the Bay and we called it. So now I get to spend it with you." He put her down and gave her a kiss on the cheek.

"That's great, Joe. I'm so glad," she said, letting him go and glancing at the muddy water pooling around his boots. "Let's do something in a bit."

"Let's do something now," he said.

"That's fine, just after I clean this up. You leave your things scattered around the house and then I spend all day getting back to normal."

He paused. "The house is always clean."

"It's clean because of me. You come and go and you're on the boat all day, and I'm just here, putting away your stuff. Is this all I am? Keeper of your things?"

"Maggie, you don't need to obsess. I don't care if the house is clean."

She looked back at the puddle.

His eyes widened in disbelief and he picked up his jacket as she made a move for it.

"Stop, Maggie."

"That's not my name."

"What's wrong with you?"

"My name's Martha."

"Okay, Martha, what's going on? You don't like Maggie all of a sudden? What does that mean?"

"I need you to listen to me," she cried, and stomped her foot.

A blood vessel in her eye burst. Red bled into blue.

Joe turned away and walked through the door he had entered moments ago, into the rain he just left, into the car that was still warm and drove down the road that was markedly more flooded than minutes before.

Martha leaned against the wall before collecting the wet gloves he had left, his work bag, the gold-plated watch he had not taken with him that morning, and drove them to the bay in silence and fog.

She navigated craggy rocks covered in algae and coarse stones that made her creep toward the water, the work bag of his belongings clamped to her chest. The freezing rain battered as she bowed her head. There was a cluster of boulders where they had picnicked on summer days when her eyes had teared from laughter and sunlight.

She stopped near a black boulder covered in white shells and orange lichen. At its base, there was an opening through which you could see sand, fine and untouched by the rain. She dug a hole and buried his effects.

Her bones ached as she plodded into the waves to her waist, gasping on contact. Remembering her bandana, she untied it from her hair and threw it to the sea, watching it blow like a petal in the wind and land between her and a struggling boat in the distance.

If it's Joe, she thought, perhaps he will pick it up for me.

loons

A paintbrush made the sky that day, the dishwater and heather grey.

Loons, she read, walk clumsily on land and their tremolos are like the laughter of a lunatic.

He called women "birds," recalling a tough old bird or a helpless Hedren.

But the things she did made sense to her.

The thought of him dripped into her lungs and sprang to her eyes.

The purple martins were out, she was happy to see. They patrol the lakefront pines with ruby-throated hummingbirds; the social and unsocial, raucous and modest, feeding on nectar or spiders or bees.

She is the loon with red eyes like banshees. She is the one who sticks her oar in the water and goes in circles.

But the things she does make sense to her.

relic/fetish

I also know that it was not you who ate
the idea, but the idea that ate you…

—Dostoevsky, *Demons*

Symbols are symbols are symbols but is truth in the joining
or parting of tans in a tangram, fragments of a stained-
glass saint in the hands of a child looking to the heavens
for help?

Copper and cobalt and lead fall from his fingers in ecstasy
and waste. And what of the shapes he makes – the etched
and cobbled and cemented, demented form, more organic
than intended?

But animal minds live in animal men.

They gnaw on the ravaged bone of yesterday.

screaming gulls

Two old men met at a coffee shop in downtown Chicago.

"It's colder than I thought it'd be,' said Alan in the beret.

"I know, I rode my bike here," said Andrew in the flat cap.

Alan brought the coffee to his lips, his hands trembling. "Show off," he said.

"Join the club, you could do a few miles," said Andrew before pausing. "I wonder what it'll be like when I'm old."

An old woman dragged a young boy into the restroom while he squealed like 'L' train steel.

His screams grew constant and comical and the men smiled.

"It sounds like birds."

The other nodded. "Like birds at the beach."

the philosophy of not wanting those things

She sits beside the book on the bed. It is large and flat with a red square on the cover under the title, *Matisse*. In front of the red square is a woman holding her hands in her lap.

To view the image from the left, her expression is of worry. From below, her face shows care. From the right, she is angry. From above, in love.

Its chapters include "Realism and Decoration" and "Beyond Spatial Limits". Real and decorative battle for primacy like naked and nude. (We cannot be semi-barbaric.)

The red paint reaches beyond the edge of its designated shape as though bleeding through extra fiber. Maybe her heart is square. It cannot quite decide which way it should be oriented. It has no ups or downs.

Part II: Ritual

the changing room

Just outside Los Angeles, an orange haze nestled into poppies, palms, and a pyramid of quartz monzonite called Old Greyback. In the city, the morning dim was pierced by the reflections of a few skyscraper suns. From east to west, the Doric columns of dawn grew from one intersection to the next, raising the temple that is downtown.

This morning's melodic introduction contained nine variations of honking horns over the punctual curses of businessmen late to work, stuck behind waddling women with suitcases and interns bobbing and weaving against pedestrian traffic.

Francesca yawned at Wilshire and Curson beside La Brea Tar Pits and inhaled the pungent hydrogen sulfide as they bubbled.

She was not far from the Lake Pit, one of many pools collected from the Salt Lake Oil Field, from which crude oil forces itself through fissures in sedimentary beds above. For tens of thousands of years, natural asphalt travelled to the surface and became covered in layers of water and soil deposits. Ice Age animals drinking from the basin became mired by the tar beneath their feet and unable to escape. Before they decayed and sank into the earth, they attracted predators who themselves became trapped.

The asphalt stained their bones dark brown.

In the palimpsest beneath Los Angeles, the partial skeleton of a young woman later named La Brea Woman was found among the millions of fossils.

Throughout history, skulls were displayed symbolically for the masses. And in LA, a cast of La Brea Woman's fractured skull was allegedly mounted onto the remains of a Pakistani woman whose bones were dyed bronze, and whose femurs were shortened to approximate her size.

The light turned green and Francesca crossed the street as rush hour began. Locals in tennis shoes scurried past suburban girls who stomped and limped in high heels. Homeless men situated by lampposts, bus stops, or trash cans said, "Have a nice day", or "I'm hungry", or "Bless you". Commuters mustered a fraction of a smile before crumpling into a grimace, the pleas and pleasantries being homeless, too.

A shriveled woman with papery skin and toes curled over one another in bow sandals pushed a cart. Men eyed women while pretending to look at their watches. The herd diverged at a row of planters in the center of the sidewalk until the third planter in, where a crowd formed around policemen. A pair of legs in rolled-up corduroys and near-translucent feet in tattered socks stuck out from the dirt and hung over the lip of the planter. His torso and face were buried beneath the day lilies, a harvest of death.

She stared at the planter where roots and eyes lay below.

But men checked their watches and women wobbled and children pulled their mothers' hands, and rolling suitcases click-click-clicked on sidewalk cracks and it was time to go.

She finished her coffee at a park where two women bandied at the entrance.

"Look, we can sit on the bench, over at the tables, on the grass, see—there's plenty to do."

A group had gathered behind the hedges separating the playground from the recently-installed sculpture garden.

They breathed, as if a single entity, sublime exhalations like "wonderful" and "beautiful" upon the newest addition, a six-foot high mirrored house in the Prairie Box style called "Homme." The home and its reflections mesmerized visitors and locals alike. She heard a young man explain as she left that the hollowness of the installation was a testament to its anthropomorphism.

The south entrance of the theater took her through dark labyrinthine tunnels to the wings where she entered stage left. It was a quarter to seven.

"Fran, up here," Ian called her from the catwalk. "You're early."

"I couldn't sleep. Your alarm went off so I figured I might as well head over. Lighting?"

"Yeah, decided to change the gobos last minute."

She joined him on the catwalk and discussed gels and dimmers until the others arrived and got settled.

"Ready, Fran?" Ian asked, glancing at his watch.

"Yep."

"And…action."

Francesca's blood hummed in her temples like the drone of flies around a dead body or a hummingbird in a claustrophobic bloom. She imagined a saber-toothed cat sinking into the ground and the exact moment its face changed, when it knew it would not escape.

...

Blackness shrank from crimson light center stage where Woman reposed in a claw-foot bathtub, covered in mounds of bubbles. A door frame sat stage right underneath a hanging digital clock with red pixels. The time was 7am.

The contrived morning glow made her skin luminous. She inhaled deeply before her first line, her bent knees an island in the shallow sea.

"Solitude, Sorrow, Eternity!" Woman cried.

A gaunt young man in a fast-food worker's uniform approached the door and knocked loudly.

"Come in," Woman called, and Francesca pondered whether Woman was a Clarissa Dalloway or a Jane Eyre. Was she a La Brea Woman? Was she six feet tall?

"He can't hear you, he's wearing a headset," said Businessman, who strode past her bathtub and exited stage left.

"Come in!" she yelled.

The door bowed as Fast-Food Worker threw his weight against the door, broke through, and sent a few splinters flying.

Woman flinched. "Red and yellow kill a fellow."

He offered her a cinnamon roll and lingered after she accepted it, the frosting covering both their hands.

"Pretty girl," said Fast-Food Worker, who smiled with grey teeth and licked his fingers before exiting stage left.

Woman took small, polite bites of her breakfast until it was finished and the stage lights diffused honey. The clock displayed 11am.

"Apple?"

Girl entered and took an apple from her apron pocket.

"Why are you wearing an apron?" asked Woman.

"Why are you naked?" countered Girl.

"I asked you first."

"Want an apple?"

Woman took the apple and said, "I've got a plan, I've got an apple in my hand."

She let it hang over the lip of the tub. *Roots and eyes.*

"You don't have a plan. Look at me now. Indecisive in a bathtub. And how *old* you are," Girl cried accusatorily at Woman before exiting the stage.

Woman took a bite of the apple as the stage lights turned magenta and the clock read 7 pm.

"Well look at you over there, eating your apple, thinking God knows what."

A tall man in a lab coat with a stethoscope around his neck entered, "Dr. Fox" sewn in navy cursive above his breast pocket.

"My heart hurts. Why did you leave?" he yelled, gesturing wildly in the direction of the audience before wiping his ginger comb-over out of his face.

"I think you have the wrong person. Apple?" she asked, offering the half-eaten fruit in his direction.

"How can you eat an apple at a time like this? You were always like that, totally unbothered. Pink Lady, I bet. I remember everything."

"Everything?" Woman asked.

"Everything. The two of us, our dream home, two cars, two dogs, two kids. Everything," he said accusatorily.

"Can you tell me what time it is?" Woman asked, delicately biting at the top of the core. "I think my clock is off," she added, pointing to the clock above the doorframe.

"It has been over twelve hours since you got into the tub, and from what I can tell, you need more bubbles," he replied.

The bubbles dwindled and exposed more than her knees to Dr. Fox.

The lights slowly faded to indigo and her hair looked black when the clock read 11pm.

"You don't look like your photo," Businessman said accusatorily, glancing at his watch as he re-entered the stage.

"No, I wouldn't," replied Woman.

"Speak up! Are you Cindy?" Businessman shouted at her.

"No," she shouted in response.

Businessman glanced out at the audience as if he were surveying newly acquired property and, smiling and chuckling to himself, looked down at his platinum cufflinks, his Gucci loafers and shook his head.

"You Queen Jezebel, you Chopin's piano. They'd throw you out the window too."

"Yes, I think they would."

"Is that why you're wasting your life in a tub? Time is money, don't you know that?" he bellowed, flailing his arm in the direction of the clock. "Your time's off by the way," he observed calmly, "I've 11 past. You should fix it."

"I don't want to be seen; I don't want to be the wrong thing. And what if I leave, and then someone comes looking for me here?"

"So, you can't fix it? There's gotta be a button, a switch, but I'm not going to do it for you…"

Businessman walked off stage.

Woman brought her knees to her chest and watched the numbers on the clock rearrange themselves. Dawn replaced midnight, washing out the neon digits before they vanished entirely. She rested her head upon her arm that was propped on the edge, then looked out directly at the audience.

"How are you like me?"

Curtain closes, end of scene.

· · ·

"Fran, you can get out now. Dan, get the lights," Ian said.

"Sorry, man."

"Fran, let's go, you're done. Great job guys. Let's get those splinters off the stage? Thanks."

Ian jogged down the aisles of the empty house and onstage where Francesca waited for him in a dressing gown.

"What'd you think?" she asked.

"Good. It looks good, it sounds good."

He was silent as he escorted her offstage and led her down the hall.

The dressing room was a salmon-colored storm. Round light bulbs framed long mirrors and a large sofa the color of dentist office wallpaper was patched with duct tape. There were rocking chairs, bar stools, broken exit signs, costume racks, fake fruit, and make-up kits orbiting Francesca as she dried the ends of her hair with a tea towel. Ian sat in an office chair behind her.

"So, what did you really think?" she asked.

"Hey, really solid start, but you're not seeing what's there," he said cautiously.

Francesca frowned and sat in a blue plastic chair in the shape of a hand at a patio table. Ian wheeled his office chair closer to her, eagerly. A tampon on the table went unmentioned.

"We'll work through it. Look, it's a woman who's afraid to grow up. She's living in this behavioral sink she can't possibly join. Mental illness, the myth of a physical ideal, class warfare, gender inequality, they materialize and she accepts them. Over and over again. It's this never-ending cycle, right? There's no room for her, right? Platforms and promises and causes – they're squeezing her out of existence."

He paused. "You played it so passively. And if you don't get it, the audience won't get it. We need them to get this bit at the beginning, it needs to be immersive."

"It's called *Spiritual Death*, they can't get too far off the mark. Although I don't think that's what it's really about, something that big and impersonal. It's all about the squeezers and not about the squeezed."

Francesca placed her hand on the table.

"What do you think my play is about?" Ian asked with half polite curiosity, leaning back in his chair.

She paused a moment before lifting her hand to her mouth and stage-whispering, "The r-word."

A pause. A stare.

"Does it rhyme with grape?"

"The bubbles, they disappeared. Men are entering this private space – all kinds of men – she's got this manifestation of her innocent self, and perverted authority figures, it's a violation! Kind of like being in rehearsal completely naked while your boyfriend directs you," she said as she stood up, untied her belt and let the robe fall to the floor. "I could have worn a swimsuit."

He stared at her blankly with eyebrows raised. Francesca redonned the robe and scrubbed off her make-up in the mirror. He watched her for a moment in silence before leaving her to get dressed.

"I need you to act like this."

normal faults

45

The plates arrive one after another. She scrapes leftover lasagna or salad or chicken bones into a trough and puts them in a rack with a hollow crack to get clean and renew their vows of service.

There are no major changes over time in the room where they wash dishes. A stainless-steel machine, a dampness in the air that never leaves, hot porcelain and kinky hair.

When your shift is long enough, you can mark intervals of time by the changes in your posture, the span from your awakening to bending, and you know when night begins without windows.

The internal processes of a commercial dishwasher are not so different from her own. Her occupation is criticism and correction. The bowls are filthy. Her habits, improper.

After having wrecked her exterior with gluttony, slumping, and smoke breaks, she will slip and fall from the stress and strain. The old self of moments ago will be buried, the new self will emerge reformed and glittering on the inside.

She tries on a regular basis to function and do her job. But geologic phenomena are driven by heat, pressure, and a destructive impulse, one possible explanation for the mountain ranges in her mind.

Our ancient atoms will clash and distance, love and hurt, dirty and clean and dirty again.

But, tired at night, she will ask for how long.

tin man

47

He cracks open a beer, hoping to deliver bitter drops of
feeling to creaky impulses for love,

as fragile as the can he drinks from.

surface tension

48

The spinster has a drop of gin on her chin.

After a nervous sip of gimlet, a single drop dribbled from her bottom lip to her chin and made its home there like a glass wart even though she is speaking.

She is wearing foundation, concealer, blush, highlighter, eye shadow, eye liner, mascara, brow powder, brow gel, lip balm, lipstick, and setting spray.

Silk hair falls over a silk dress with a neckline that shows the beginning of cleavage, but there is a large drop of gin residing on her chin.

cleaver street

She is seam ripping in the living room. She is right-handed
and methodical, pausing to plan her attack, eyes narrowed,
finding the few black threads among the grey and white.
She stabs herself only once, and at the end, because she
was still thinking of him like the seam so brutally torn
from its fellow.

She lives across from a church and there seems to be a
blue sky behind it even on winter days. Her brain edits out
the telephone wires that split the rose window in half and
the inconvenient smog. It would be unpleasant to
acknowledge them, but she knows it's necessary to be
reminded, on occasion, of the things in front of us we
prefer not to see.

She is in the kitchen chopping vegetables. She is in the
hallway doing yoga.

We ignite hand-rolled cigarettes with the word
"Revelation" and our hair floats out the bathroom window
with the smoke.

I am beside the ofrenda hemming a sweater. I listen to the rain tap Morse code on our windowsill with Mahler playing through the vents and wonder if she recognizes the tune.

I've lived here for one year. She's lived here for one year before me.

I wonder, at times, if we are a past and future iteration of the other. The differences between us are few. But how can I be her when she is already so close to being me? When I cannot tell what time has changed between us? When I can only measure current closeness as an approximation for being?

"W

ater Street

maybe, if you know

Michigan Ave don't have."

"Anybody have change for a

bite to eat or some coffee?" "Anybody

have change for a bite to eat or some coffee?"

"Anybody have change for a bite to eat or some

coffee?"   Repeated over and over in a soft, uncertain

voice as if someone had taught him to recite those words

precisely and

politely forever.

He might've

been a hunter,

but he's gathering

g

o

o

d

n

e

s

s

an occasional problem in customer service

52

"Hi, is this Keith?"

"No, this is Keith."

the oppressive constant of taking

53

The melancholic cornflowers are swollen with penny-
water, stolen from the golden rolling hills that swallowed
me whole 'til I emerged, blooms in hand, from that fertile
sea whose thorns pricked my fingers and made them bleed;

and when I came home and looked back at those yellow
weeds swaying, menacingly, in the breeze, my eyes paused
on the fig tree among them and the blackbird gripping a
branch with dark claws before launching himself into the
sky, flying in circles, making his way toward the apricot
tree

beside my window, pecking at the fruit, his beak
frustratedly piercing the bark around its target of orange
flesh, croaking occasionally as if to beg reprieve from the
winds that blew, the winds that threw him to another
branch, another tree,

and I refilled the vase as I reflected on the gracelessness of
pleasure.

the omelette

54

And when he begins to stir in bed, she ends her recollections of younger days, her fondnesses and caprices and dreams of Myrna Loy, and, setting down her tea, begins her constitutional around the kitchen, considering whether to make an omelette or crêpes for breakfast and whether to serve strawberries and pears fresh or in a compôte.

She wipes down the kitchen methodically beginning with the nearest counter and working clockwise, reciting a psalm for every surface.

Once the humble egg is transformed into the sophisticated omelette, she adds a sprinkle of fleur de sel and places it at the head of the table beside a small bowl of fruit.

Her palms are beside one another in the sink as if splaying the Bible out on its back while she lets the soap erase any impurity that longing for past years may have sown.

After she folds a napkin, fills a cup with black coffee, and
sits down, she rearranges a curl that had come loose from
her barrette and lets out an audible sigh.

One day, you will need what you need. And still, it is
unfair.

heavy pots

When I was little, my mother told me, "One day, you will be able to pick up heavy pots."

I marveled that her bare hands held scalding pot handles as if it were nothing while she served us dinner.

One day I will wonder, "Did they love me, or did they love what I did for them?"

Part III: Refrain

primitive comfort

On Sundays, the prairie is huddled close to the ground to better hear the orchestral clack of dead leaves on silphium stalks, the hollow clangs of a carillon, exhales of beloved skeletons.

Bones buried on top of one another like telephone poles shrinking in the distance, like sins overlapping a lifetime.

On Sundays, mist like breath rises in the native grass. Sensing a transcendental change in state, seagulls hover like white kites and gray gales flip gold coins in cottonwoods.

Exhale as I describe to her the wheat like silver tassels and goldenrod pagodas as if she were only blind and not gone.

still life

Is it dirt or is it shadow smeared across the canvas, lemons
with dark leaves, mallards with curled claws?

The painter hung it on the wall and languished in its
artlessness and candor.

A feather, skull, a bit of twine, a breast upon which dust
collects, with wings upside-down and askew and confused
in their new nature.

They cannot land and cannot fall, but hang where they are
hung, their eyes closed, their necks touching one another
like the stems of a bouquet.

abilene

On summer days, kicking gravel under cigarette smoke and
floodlights buzzing with electric moths, she rose at dawn
to tend the horses, the goats, the sheep, and the cattle dogs
called Sunny and Two-Step.

Named for where her mother's car broke down from the
heat, they settled dreaming of gold on roads with potholes.
Behind them, rank and file pecan trees reach for purple
mountains like soldiers saluting the sky.

She lived on shag carpet in velvet robes and sequin belts,
shooting squirrels out front with a Colt pistol from a
wicker chair lined with cobwebs and brown recluses
periodically beaten back by her nurse who sang in Spanish
with cracks in her voice like those in the foundation of the
abandoned gas station next door through which yellow
poppies sprang and bent in the onslaught of dust from the
foothills they fled.

#573

The nurse worked the night shift and shouldn't have been there, it's just that someone had called off, so she wouldn't know where to expect Elsie at this hour of the day. She was pregnant and working into the early afternoon, ambling in camo clogs and apologizing for not knowing where to find an old woman with a failing memory.

A 90s thriller was on the television in the sitting room, affixed before a balding woman in a wheelchair by a fake fireplace, surrounded by bookshelves filled with 70s paperbacks in small print, and she listened in as the nurse spoke on the phone with her sister about the unfortunate scheduling, her back hurting, and needing to look for an independent-living woman.

The corkboard wall behind her desk was littered with daily routine checklists and the names of two women who were hospice, DNR, comfortable bedding and soothing sounds because, per the posted literature, vision was the first thing to go, becoming glazed and far away. But hearing continues until the end, and I found it reassuring that one day if my mother could not see me, she could hear my apologies and thanks for mistakes and good times.

The nurse walked me down the length of the L-shaped complex from assisted to independent living. Right at the inner corner there was a bird cage at the bottom of a staircase that swept out like the skirt of a ballgown. It was full of finches with bright beaks and rosy cheeks and small, round chirps that recalled woods of dappled emerald light.

It was across from a row of aquariums in the darkest outer corner of the building, with fluorescent blue light, the faint gurgling of water, and the angel fish and guppies and swordtails, platies and mollies and tetras and one large, bloated loach sitting at the bottom like the man in front of the tank, who slid down in his wheelchair with hunched shoulders.

Elsie Beech is in her room, #573, with a large gold doorstop in the shape of a seal, who welcomes me in, and offers me tea, and a book by Flannery.

the haunting of a chess piece by patsy cline

Words creep like chess pieces incrementally toward their objective. Expressions of love manifest a drunken line dance across the files; grief reverberates across the board as heartbroken pawns wear a stiff upper lip. Some resolve to be sacrificed for the greater good, the desperados of every rank. The king is quiet and wants to be left alone.

For a time, the center of the board librates, occasionally bringing rivals close enough to touch only to pause at recognition of themselves in the other, uncertain of their intent.

But they rejoin the fray, boxwood and rosewood, the queen beginning her ascent to the throne like a model down the runway; the bristling knights and dumpy rooks fawn over her, the bishop eyes her surreptitiously from beneath his mitre.

The queen, of course, is Patsy Cline – all beaming sorrow and joy in equal measure – who sings:

it's okay, it's okay, me too!

The tragedy is not in the last king's reign coming to a close.

It is in the premature death of the queen who moves us.

anke's ataraxia

The human body is fragile and Walter Cobbe was unlucky.
The private jet he flew himself entered aerodynamic stall
and crashed into a retention pond behind a supermarket.

The plane that carried him in his final moments was called
a bizjet despite his lifelong disdain for conducting
business. He had, along with all known forebears, inherited
great wealth that required little personal intervention to
maintain.

An imposing figure at 6'5", Cobbe travelled from one
metropolis to another. Not even his secretary knew what
these jaunts entailed, why he always travelled alone, barely
the date of his possible return, although she suspected he
endeared himself to multiple women.

He was an effervescent man of means and seemed beloved
by all he met. It was as if every acquaintance received,
instead of a business card, a memorable encounter to hold
close and retell. Cobbe believed he was one of the few to
ever live who knew exactly when to listen and exactly
when to speak.

On one occasion, he listened for an hour with a pleasant expression on his face, of genuine interest and enjoyment, to a woman outside the post office describing her upcoming retirement. It concluded with a timely wink and well-wish.

Another night, he had listened to a man recall his mother's last words on her deathbed, and bestowed upon him, suddenly, an arm around the shoulder, squeeze, and a couple pats on the back. He told the man his mother also died, although he wasn't there to hear her last words.

His grey eyes were hidden behind wearied folds of flesh following the discovery of his downed plane. A sterile white cover strapped his ample girth to a stretcher as the medical examiner determined Cobbe had untreated hypertension and a ruptured aortic aneurysm.

...

Anke's face shown bluish-green from the TV screen. Her dark brown hair frizzed at the edges and caught the afternoon light while chubby fingers stumbled across the edges of an apple sticker marked "Ambrosia."

"Anke, where are your shoes? TV off, please, and pick some flowers."

Lydia watched as her daughter peeled a label off an apple in the center of the den. A mass of tangled curls framed big grey eyes hidden with the concentration of removing smudges. Lydia joined her on the floor.

"See the ladybug? On the sticker?"

Anke's gaze shifted from the apple to the curled sticker resting on the tips of shag carpet. *#3507* was typed above the image of a small ladybug.

"They're a gift from God, named for Our Lady. They're supposed to bring us good luck."

Anke did not, in Lydia's opinion, need to learn words associated with financial hardship. If she did not have the vocabulary, she could not express the concept, and would not know the sting of associating scarcity with oneself.

Anke went to her room and Lydia fumbled about in her purse. Keys, wallet, perfume sample, loose change, and finally the squashed package of Camel Straights.

"Almost ready, bud?"

She stationed herself at the edge of the patio beneath the floodlight decoupaged with moth bodies.

Lydia took her final drag beside the chimney and watched as Anke took the rusty shears left perennially in the garden and cut a few stalks of yarrow before skipping back to the patio.

Something was wrong with her mother. The shoulder length blonde hair that was usually wavy had been smoothed to a dull sheen and braided lifelessly beside her neck. Her rosy complexion was replaced with a certain ruddiness in the cheeks that bracketed a frown as she held out her hand.

"Let's go. Don't want to be late."

...

The funeral service took place on the Cobbe estate. A banal, neatly attended landscape stretched for acres in each direction until it met the perfectly square iron enclosure of the family plot.

At the north entrance, two weeping willows looked like great wrists bent backwards with fingers frozen in an upward curl.

The branches from the border of bur oak and yew suggested the edges of a cube, as if the dead slept in a greenhouse with its own dew, its own earth and shade, where visitors walk gently.

Inside was an ostentatious jumble of obelisks and mausoleums and headstones, wisteria clutching decayed trunks, a retaining wall halfway sunken underground, and Johnny jump-ups covering a few modest mounds of earth.

His body was to be laid in the southwest corner of the plot beside the cenotaph of his mother, Anne.

The service itself was held in the estate's replica of the Gothic Revival Leeds Cathedral that loomed above the manicured countryside.

Lydia drove up the newly sealed asphalt road and parked in the west lot of the church. Their smoky skirted suit and small daffodil dress approached the threshold and a young man gave Lydia a pamphlet. On the front was an image of Walter Cobbe that read, "Why do the righteous suffer?"

Mother and daughter walked solemnly into the nave. Anke joined the throng mourning Cobbe, holding the bouquet of yarrow in front of her politely.

Lydia stuck to the west wall, observing the crowd that had assembled for Walter. Every once in a while, she saw her daughter shift between pews and people of importance.

Anke weaved through the grove of stockinged and slacked legs, lightly brushing up against their fabrics. Satin and silk and chiffon hems caught her hair, batiste cotton blends gentle against her fingertips. Stiff brocade scarves draped to the floor. Denim and moleskin met seersucker abruptly as the tone of conversation changed.

"What are you drinking?" a woman asked.

A shrill voice responded. "Borjomi. Volcanic spring water. Supposedly therapeutic. Vacationed in Tbilisi – nightmare. No amenities, nothing. Anyway, the water's supposed to be brilliant. Have a sip."

A pause. Her hand covered her mouth, tittering, "I can't believe you're drinking dirty sock water."

"Nothing better, darling."

A voice like gravel began, "So he said to him, 'There's nothing sadder than a grown man who can't support himself.' I was sitting on a bench, he comes up to me, towering over me, asks me how I plan to get clean. Don't know how he knew I had my problems but guess I looked the part. 'I drink tea,' I said. 'Religiously.' He laughed so hard. Grabbed me by the collar, slapped me on the back, and put me in his '59 Eldorado Biarritz. Never seen anything so beautiful. And he was smiling the whole time, like he was laughing at life, or laughing at how happy I was. Asked all about me, how I grew up, what my family was like. 120 on the off-roads—"

"Why do the righteous suffer, Father?" a woman asked, pleading.

"God makes the righteous suffer for their betterment. He hones our virtues in that He might…"

"It was just six months ago," a twenty-something in a bow tie began, already reveling in his story, "I contacted his secretary, Cat, explained I was interested in interviewing him. Naturally, since he's one of the few remaining Cobbes, I wanted an oral history. Two months later he returns my call. He's not interested. I ask why. He says the world doesn't need another account of a wealthy family with a stupid last name. Could not believe it."

Jokingly, "Wise old man who wouldn't say anything. Asshole." Nervous laughter.

Accents and volumes blended together as if the entire social stratosphere were harmonizing. Anke made her way to the easel cradling the framed oil on canvas countenance of a younger Walter Cobbe. His mustache bristled with the indignity of sitting for hours, his eyes demanded release at the recognition of an artist who painted a subject's interiority instead of simply their defining physical features.

This artist was supremely talented, having been a beneficiary of Cobbe patronage. He captured a certain set of his brow and clenched jaw alluding to his intransigence and the slightest upturn in his mouth that, paired with a glint in his eyes, hinted to the capricious nature that drove his associations.

A whim, once decided upon, was pursued whole-heartedly, but he always left, quite abruptly, at the first sign of someone forming a negative opinion of him. He couldn't face anyone he had let down, and why should he if he didn't have to. Acquaintances were permeable to his charm and safe from his moods. With new faces came new opportunities to be the man he would consider becoming permanently, when conditions were optimal.

It pained him, sometimes, to think his motivations were selfish.

Moments later, he would admit graciously that that was just the way he was, and that was the end of it.

Anke peered up at the closed casket, propped the twined yarrow on its edge, and returned to her mother.

Lydia was leaning awkwardly against a stone pillar, clutching her purse to her stomach and blankly observing the crowd. High society women, girls half her age. Old men, old money, no money. And herself, a forty-something whose makeup was already settling in the creases of her face, the rose eye shadow burrowing into the folds of her eyelids and making tiny streaks like the contrails of a jet at sunset.

It had always seemed to her that the moments that should have been the greatest – the moments for which she styled her hair and dabbed perfume on her wrists and took extra care in dressing – had always been interrupted by the callousness of others like—

"Walter Cobbe," the priest began, "was a man of greatness. A man whose kindness flowed freely, a man whose eyes shown with love for the Lord."

Walter Cobbe and the few remaining Cobbes were atheists. The stained-glass windows of cartoon disciples had always recalled to him a kaleidoscope, light and shadow flung haphazardly onto walls of worship. Men and women in the hands of an angry god finding relief in tessellation, dangling from a thread of their own fraying.

"Psalm 23 reads, 'He makes me lie down in green pastures; He leads me beside quiet waters.' Truly God has helped Cobbe lead a life of financial success and generosity, of discernment and wise words. He lived a remarkably full life whose joy he shared with everyone around him. I would like to thank you all for coming to celebrate the righteous life of Walter Cobbe and invite those who knew him best to share a few words."

Catherine approached the altar.

"I worked for Walter for nearly 15 years."

She cleared her throat.

"He gave me a job when I needed one desperately, and for that I'm grateful. He played an important role in my life and my family's life and your lives as well, I'm sure," she trembled as looked out at the audience. "But it's important to be honest about who he was, the legacy he leaves behind. Walter could see what's right for everyone but himself. It was hard to really know him. I don't know that there's a single person here who really knew him, after his mother passed."

She paused.

"But he wasn't a great man."

A collective gasp echoed from the pews. They glared, as one entity, at the surely bitter, likely-rebuffed woman, and enjoyed the sense of importance that comes from taking secondhand offense.

"He never stuck around."

At this last thought, she briefly made eye contact with Lydia and walked briskly out of the church, head down.

Lydia let out an exhale locked deep inside her. But cleaning a countertop in the kitchen does not lift the stain in the living room.

A suited porcine man holding a flask stood up and shuffled toward the stage.

"If Walt were here, he'd tell me to get on with it, so we could drink after the service. I'll keep this short…"

Everyone laughed, and Anke laughed with them, and Lydia took her hand and led her outside and they got in the car.

love hearts

"Art. Art?"

Arthur was deep in thought.

He wondered how to prevent being lost in time with no one to remember his name. He was average and unlikely to do great things that would warrant recognition or remembrance.

And on top of everything, she was leaving and then he would only be called *Arthur.*

His throat began to close and his eyes began to water. He pushed his glasses further up the bridge of his nose and swallowed the sadness left unspoken. He was no man. He had no voice.

"Are you okay? I have to go."

He looked at her over the earthenware vase between them holding a single daisy. The stems of their water glasses

caught the light of the morning sun and looked like
candles frozen in a flicker.

The scrape of a chair moving away from him preceded the
whistle of the train and he looked out the window. Her
hair blew beautifully in the wind, he thought, and was glad
he couldn't see her face.

Well, that's that…

What kind of heart could wrench itself from me?

refraction

Missouri, 1990. My husband's only swimming lesson.

He paddled in the flock of water wings when the lifeguard blew her whistle and pointed to the high board. It would break fear and build courage, as it had always done.

While boys lined the ladder, he floated and let their happy treble tones lap his bones.

She blew her whistle a second and third time and he shed the wings and walked trembling to the high board. His toes curled over the edge that was intractable and he replayed the directive that was undeniable. It had begun to rain. He leapt.

And sank. Her cheery affirmations were as bent as the braces on her teeth or the frayed hem of gravity around earth. Before he was retrieved, he reached for braids of sunlight on blue tile.

...

Missouri, 2020. His remains found in the St. Francis River.

Prehistoric in its accidentality, picturesque as a Civil War photo.

I went to live with my mother and she took his place at the far end of the dining table where orange candlelight flickered against her frizzy red hair.

With wine lipstick and pale complexion, she looked almost Elizabethan and, while I mourned, she read me *The Tempest* through a locked door. Sometimes, she even spoke like a character in a play, pithy and poignant, entranced by her own words, oblivious to her audience.

When you're underwater, she tells me, you know exactly where to go.

a reminder to myself

81

We are not born weak or powerful.

We become weak or powerful.

out of many, one

The air is idle-mild and the grass is mangled-cut. The
clouds are cotton balls ripped apart by long, acrylic nails
hell-bent on economy.

America is the one who commits crimes called passion and
the one who is quiet and complicit.

She is grief by the sea in a blue-hour blouse and seaweed
skirt and thin black belt.

This is not what I had dreamt.

Her ancestors gone, she faces the task of sorting her loved
ones' belongings into things to treasure, things to donate,
and things to toss. She will work long hours. She will sing
old hymns.

Twilight fades and lamplight smudges ochre on black
waves. Boats shine like beams in pinhole cameras. Dogs
bark and Irish music is playing somewhere.

Lemon and lime and pink grapefruit-colored lights twinkle from the Ferris wheel in the distance and, in that impulsive moment, among drunk happy voices and her own dim reflection, she pledges allegiance to an angry inheritance.

But because she loves her, she will pretend to love her until she loves her again.

The End

Cecelia lives in Chicago with her cat, Pooka.

www.ingramcontent.com/pod-product-compliance
Lightning Source LLC
Chambersburg PA
CBHW020049310726
48970CB00007B/2483